little Miss Wise

by Roger Hargreaves

D1324122

Little Miss Wise was as wise as an owl.

Possibly two owls.

Being so wise and sensible meant
that Little Miss Wise
brushed her teeth every day,
made her bed every day,
tidied her house every day,
and did lots of other
wise and sensible things.

If you are as wise as Little Miss Wise,
you'll know just what kind of other things she did.

Little Miss Wise liked to go for a walk
every day.

A walk that was neither too long, nor too short.

A walk that was wise and sensible.

Or sensible and wise, if you prefer.

On her walks she often met other people.

People who were not quite so wise.

And sometimes, people who were decidely unwise.

Last Monday she met Little Miss Naughty.

"Come and jump in the puddles!"
cried Little Miss Naughty,
with a naughty gleam in her eye.

But Little Miss Wise,
being wise,
refused.

She didn't want to get HER feet wet.

On Tuesday she met Little Miss Greedy,
who was carrying an enormous cake filled
with cream and smothered with pink icing.

"Would you like some of this?"
asked Little Miss Greedy.

Little Miss Wise refused.

She didn't want an upset stomach.

On Wednesday Little Miss Wise refused to get into Mr Busy's racing car.

She didn't want to have an accident.

On Thursday she refused to go into
Mr Messy's house.

"If I go into his house I will get dirty,"
she said to herself.

But she didn't say anything to Mr Messy.

She didn't want to hurt his feelings.

On Friday she refused to
play tennis with Mr Silly.

There's nothing silly about that,
is there?

By Saturday, Little Miss Wise was feeling unhappy.

"If I keep saying 'no' all the time, I'll upset everybody and I won't have any friends left," she said to herself.

She thought long and hard about the problem, and being the wise and sensible person she is, she came up with an answer.

"From now on, I will say 'yes' to everything."

On Sunday, while she was out on one of her wise and sensible walks, or sensible and wise walks, if you prefer, Little Miss Wise met Mr Mischief.

He was carrying a parcel.

"Please accept this small present," he said to her.

"N..." began Little Miss Wise.
but then she remembered her decision.

"Yes! Thank you!" she cried.

She took the parcel.

And off skipped Mr Mischief
with a mischievous grin on his face.

Little Miss Wise opened the parcel.

"ATISHOO!" she sneezed.

Then she sneezed again.

And she sneezed, and sneezed, and sneezed
all day long.

She used 199 handkerchiefs.

Mr Mischief's present
had been sneezing powder!

Today is Monday and Little Miss Wise
has stopped sneezing.

She is on one of her wise and sensible walks,
or sensible and wise walks, if you prefer,
and she has met Mr Nonsense.

"Would you like to ride in my aeroplane?" he asks.

"N..." Little Miss Wise starts to say.

But then she changes her mind and exclaims:
"Oh, yes please!"

You think she is being very unwise, don't you?
You think she should have learnt her
lesson by now, don't you?

Well she is safe this time.

Because Mr Nonsense's aeroplane
doesn't have any wings,
or an engine,
or even wheels.

It's just a doormat.

Have you ever heard of such nonsense!

Only need a few Little Miss or Mr. Men to complete your set? You can order any of the titles on the back of the books from our Mr. Men order line on 0870 787 1724. Orders should be delivered between 5 and 7 working days.